My Sister's Wedding

A Story of Kenya

I dedicate this book to the memory of my beloved parents, Mbuthia Mucheru and Wanjira Mbuthia Mucheru, who left their children the priceless gifts of industry and work ethics, and taught them the true meaning of parenthood and altruism; to my children, KK, Njeri and Njira; to my husband, Tom: Thank you for your loyal and loving support; and last but not least, many thanks to my friend, Ngugi wa Thiongo, for recommending me to Soundprints for this project. —W.M.

To my loving wife, Nungari, and my son, Karanja, for their encouragement and support —G.G.K.

Published by Soundprints, an imprint of Trudy Corporation, Norwalk, Connecticut.

www.soundprints.com

Book layout: Marcin D. Pilchowski
Editor: Laura Gates Galvin
Editorial assistance: Chelsea Shriver

First Edition 2002
10 9 8 7 6 5 4 3 2
Printed in China

Library of Congress Cataloging-in-Publication Data is on file with the publisher and the Library of Congress.

My Sister's Wedding

A Story of Kenya

by Waithira Mbuthia   Illustrated by Geoffrey Gacheru Karanja

Soundprints®
Where Children Discover...

My sister, Wangari, is going to marry Munene. Tonight, I lie in bed and think about how much I will miss her.

I will miss sitting with her in our usual place under the tree. She and I talk while I braid her hair.

My sister and I sing songs and tell riddles. We take long walks through the village. She taught me how to make a doll out of sticks and banana leaves.

I will miss her bedtime stories and the way she comforts me when thunder and lightning fill our pitch-black room. I fall asleep tonight thinking how different my life will be.

Today, my aunts and Wangari's friends help her pack all the clothes she has received from relatives and friends. One of my aunts sings a song: "Forty cows, sheep and goats to get our beautiful daughter."

This is the dowry that Munene's family has given for Wangari. "How many did you say?" we all sing.

"Forty fat big ones, for a special girl," my aunt sings back.

Then we all cheer and hug Wangari.

14

Later, my sister takes me aside. "Wambui, I want you to have something."

I tell myself I will not cry. I am a big girl of ten. But tears cloud my eyes when I see the beautiful beaded necklace she has given me.

"It's all right, little sister." Wangari wipes the tears away. "You know I love you."

Today, I am up with the sun. All is ready. Today is the wedding! But I cannot give away the secret. Wangari doesn't know yet. That is the custom of our people. The wedding day is a surprise for the bride.

Wangari leaves with Munene's mother to dig yams. In the garden, Munene's mother says, "Wangari, I forgot my special machete," and she disappears. Then she calls to some women hiding behind the banana leaves.

The women pick up Wangari, carrying her shoulder-high, and begin walking toward Munene's home. Wangari realizes what is happening. "Where are you taking me?" she asks, but she knows she is going to her new home.

Many people line the way to Munene's home, cheering the bride. At her new house, family and friends welcome Wangari with songs and cheers. We sing and dance and eat the delicious food waiting for us!

At the end of the party, each of Wangari's friends gives her a gift. I am her special helper. As each person hands Wangari a gift, she passes it to me. I give it to a woman who puts it in a special place.

As the friends bring the gifts, they sing *kiriro* songs. The songs say that even if her friends are sad that Wangari is leaving, they are still happy for her.

I am happy for her, too. The *kiriro* songs will last for eight days. In ten days, Wangari will be back for our parents' blessing. I will give her the bracelet and ring I have made with tiny beads.

28

Tonight I lie in bed and think about my sister.
I hear loud thunder and see the lightning light up
my pitch-black room. Then I hear my sister's soft
voice say, "You'll be fine, Wambui, you'll see."
And I fall asleep knowing that she is right.

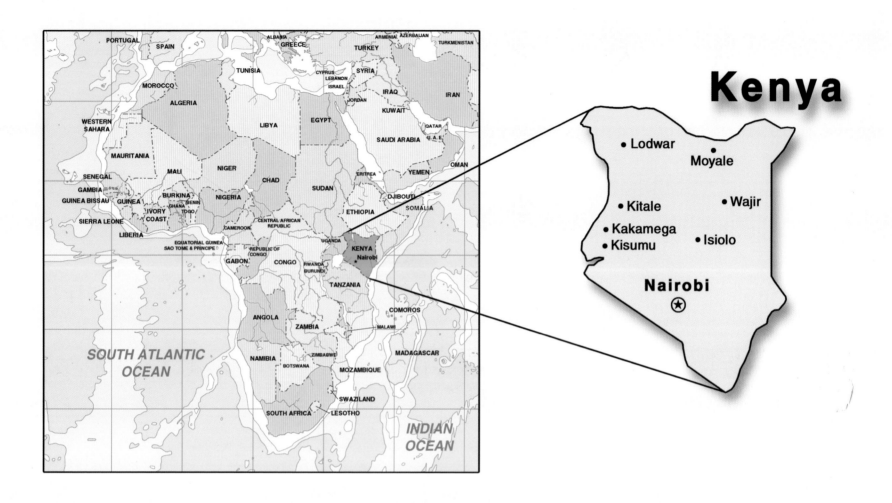

About Kenya

Located in the heart of Africa, Kenya shares a border with Ethiopia and Sudan to the north, Uganda to the west, Tanzania to the south and the Indian Ocean to the east. Kenya is home to arid northern deserts, lush savannahs, coastal lowlands and highlands. Kenya is famous for being one of Africa's major safari and tourist destinations, as well as being "the cradle of humanity." In areas of the Great Rift Valley, scientists have discovered some of the earliest evidence of man's ancestors. In the present day, Kenya's ethnic diversity has produced a vibrant culture. There are more than 70 different ethnic groups among the Africans in Kenya. The Gikuyu people featured in this story are the largest single ethnic group in Kenya. The population of Kenya is over 30 million and about 4 million people speak Gikuyu.

About the Gikuyu Wedding

The wedding in this story takes place within a community of people called Gikuyu. The Gikuyu people are very close and know each other very well from the time they are young children.

Every Gikuyu child belongs to a group with which he or she grows up. Therefore, when a boy is interested in marrying a girl, there is no need for courting. Instead, he approaches the girl and her family. If she accepts him, the boy's parents then prepare for *njohi ya njooria*—a ceremony that is performed with beer being drunk from a special horn by the girl, family and friends to announce the engagement.

Before a wedding takes place, two other ceremonies are performed—*ngoima ya ngurario*, a ceremony of purification and protection, and *guthinja ngoima*, a ceremony of signing the marriage contract. From here on the girl is regarded as blessed and given to the boy's family by her parents. She can then be taken at any time for her "surprise wedding day!"

Here are some words that you might hear spoken in Kenya today:

wĩmwega: hello.

thiĩ na wega: goodbye.

maitũ: mother.

baba: father.

mwarĩ wa maitũ: my sister.

ũhiki: wedding.

kĩnjinji: village.

kĩheo: gift.

rwĩmbo: song or dance.

kũina: to sing.